DON'T CALL ME SLOB-O

DORIS ORGEL
Illustrated by BOB DORSEY

Bank Street

Hyperion Paperbacks for Children
New York

First Hyperion Paperback edition 1996
Text ©1996 by Bank Street College of Education.
Illustrations © 1996 by Bob Dorsey.
For information address Hyperion Books for Children, 114 Fifth Avenue, New York, New York 10011-5690.
Printed in the United States of America.
First Edition
1 3 5 7 9 10 8 6 4 2
The artwork for this book is prepared using pencil.
The text for this book is set in 12-point Berling.

Library of Congress Cataloging-in-Publication Data
Orgel, Doris
    Don't call me slob-o / by Doris Orgel.
        p.   cm. — (The West Side Kids; 2)
    Summary: Shrimp must decide whether to befriend the new boy in his neighborhood, who is a Croatian American, or to join the kids who make fun of his name and accent.
        ISBN 0-7868-2086-1 (lib. bdg.) — ISBN 0-7868-1044-0 (pbk.)
        [1. Croatian Americans—Fiction. 2. Popularity—Fiction.
3. Friendship—Fiction. 4. City and town life—Fiction.]
I. Title. II. Series.
PZ7.0632Ki 1996
[Fic]—dc20   95-4822

Other books in the West Side Kids series

The Big Idea

For Willy
—D. O.

CONTENTS

THE WEST SIDE KIDS' NEIGHBORHOOD

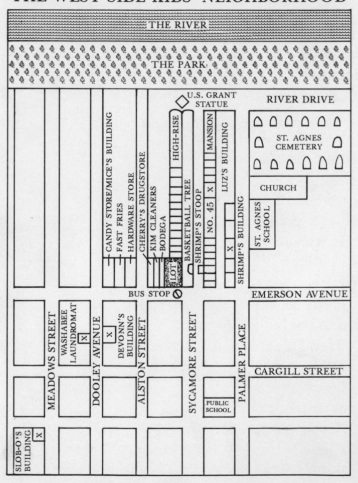

ONE-ON-NONE

I'M SHORT. Kids call me "Shrimp." Every time we choose up teams, I get chosen last. Or else I'm odd kid out.

Like what happened on Sunday, the last day of spring vacation.

I was down at the end of Sixth Street, over by the big tree with the crooked branch. It's great for shooting baskets. Well, there's no basket. But the branch is just the right height. What you do is, you loop the ball over that branch.

There was no one else around. I started playing one-on-none. It's not that much fun, but I needed the practice.

Pretty soon, DeVonn Chapman came along. I was glad to see him.

"Hey, DeVonn, want to play?" I called.

DeVonn said, "Sure."

I went first, and I did all right—sank two in a row, right smack over the branch.

"Good going," I thought DeVonn might say. Or, "You've improved." Or something like that.

But he didn't even notice. He turned the other way and yelled, "Yo, Mike!"

It was Mike Donnelly, walking like he owned the whole street. That's the kind of kid he is.

I dribbled the ball toward the tree to take another shot. Mike grabbed it away like it was his. He aimed.

"Watch this!" he said. And he missed.

Even so, the same old thing happened that always happens. I was out of the game, just like that.

I plunked myself down on the third step of the stoop at the end of the street. That step was going to have a hollow place shaped like my behind, from all the time I sat there alone.

I watched the other guys play.

I've known both of them practically forever. We met in kindergarten. Back then we were all little shrimps, not just me. So they didn't call me Shrimp yet. But they had enough fun with my real name—which, would you believe, happens to be Filomeno. You can imagine what they did with that: Mean-oh, Meanie, Wilhelmina. . . . It's a long, long list.

And my last name, Pazzalini, is not exactly tease-proof either.

My mom says my name sounds like music. She loves it. She says that when kids tease me about it, I should just ignore them. Sure. Thanks for the advice, Mom. I tried. It worked about as well as ignoring a bad case of hiccups or a pointy pebble in your shoe.

Anyway, by first grade all the other kids were way taller than me. So they started calling me Shrimp.

One time when my mom heard kids tease me about my size, she bent down and kissed me on top of my head. I was glad nobody was looking, or I would have never lived it down.

My mom can be pretty embarrassing sometimes.

Right now she's in Florida, taking care of Great-aunt Angie. The first few days were kind of fun, just Dad and me on our own. But she's been gone almost a whole week. And I miss her. I wish Great-aunt Angie would get better soon so Mom could hurry up and come home.

Sitting on my stoop, watching Mike and DeVonn throw the ball, I thought of another thing Mom said when she heard kids teasing me. "Never mind. Shrimps can turn into giants." She writes poems, that's how she gets those ideas.

Shrimp into giant . . . wouldn't that be neat? Like, when I got up off the stoop, I'd suddenly be a foot or two taller than Mike and DeVonn. . . . "Excuse me," I would say politely. Then I'd grab the ball out of Mike's clutches, reach up, and not even throw it, just dunk it over the branch . . . yeah!

Too bad things like that never happen in real life.

I got sick of watching. I stood up.

"So long, guys, I'm going home." I held out my arms. But they'd forgotten all about that it was my ball and kept on playing.

Just then this totally strange-looking kid came around the corner. He was almost as tall as a grown-up but gawky and skinny. His pants were way too big on him. They bunched up around his waist like on a scarecrow. His hair was jagged, like whoever cut it used scissors that weren't sharp. Some of it fell over his forehead. He kept his head down, looking at the sidewalk. What I saw of his face was pale, like he never got out in the sun.

The ball went rolling toward him.

Mike ran for it and nearly knocked him over. "Hey, creep, watch where you're going!"

The kid jumped out of the way, over to the edge of the sidewalk near where I was standing. He blinked a lot, like he was scared, not sure what to do. Then he clutched at something dangling from a string around his neck and stuck it, quick, under his shirt.

I said, "Hi," and took a step toward him.

He froze. He stood there with his hands out in front of him—like to defend himself. Did he think I was going to hit him?

I laughed. I couldn't help it. He probably thought I was laughing at him. But, that wasn't it at all. The reason I laughed was I suddenly got this great idea. Hey, here's the chance I've been waiting for!

TWO-ON-TWO

I HELD OUT my hand. The kid just stood there. I stuck my hand out farther and said, "Shake?"

So we did. Then I pulled him over to Mike and DeVonn.

"Who's this creep?" said Mike.

"Friend of yours, Shrimp?" asked DeVonn.

I shrugged. "Never saw him before. Hey, kid, what's your name?"

He stared down at the pavement and mumbled something.

"What?" said Mike. "We didn't catch that."

The kid repeated what he'd mumbled, "Slbb-bllb-dlln" or something like that.

"He can't talk too well," DeVonn said.

"He can talk all right," said Mike. "But maybe it's moon language. Am I right? Is that where you come from, the moon?"

The kid scrunched his eyebrows together and shook his head.

"Oh, sorry. You come from farther out," said Mike. "I know, outer space!"

The kid made fists.

I don't know if he understood the words, but I think he could tell they weren't nice.

"Well then, where *are* you from?" DeVonn asked.

"Split."

Mike made a face. "Where's that?"

"I never heard of it," DeVonn said.

Mike said, "Tell you what: Why don't you go back there? I mean, why don't you split, ha-ha!"

DeVonn joined in. "Yeah, right, ha-ha."

I laughed, too, to keep them company. But I felt kind of bad doing it.

DeVonn had the ball. He threw it to Mike. "Your turn. Go on, shoot."

I jumped up and down in front of Mike, waving my arms to guard him. "Hold it," I said, "why don't we let him play?"

"We?" Mike gave me a stare, like I had some nerve to want to be in on their game.

"Aw, give Shrimp a break. It's his ball," DeVonn said. "I say, let's ask the guy. That way Shrimp can play, too."

I felt like shouting, "Yay, hurray!" But I stayed cool, as if I didn't really care.

Mike thought it over. Suddenly, *wham*, he threw the ball at the strange kid. It hit him in the stomach and bounced down the sidewalk.

The kid doubled over.

"Come on, get the ball," I yelled.

And after a second he did. He went for it and started trying to dribble.

Mike tapped him on the shoulder. "Okay. You and me against them. At least you're tall. You shouldn't do too bad. Know how to play?"

The strange kid said, "Is basketball? But where is basket?"

We started explaining, "See that branch? The ball has to go over it. Every time it does, your team gets a point."

"Branch? Is basket?" The kid looked blank.

"We better show him." DeVonn motioned to the kid to throw him the ball.

He threw it. But not to DeVonn, to me. I caught it, just barely. I felt jittery all over. I was sure I'd miss the branch by a mile. Then Mike would change his mind and say "Forget it!" And the whole thing wouldn't happen.

I walked over to take my shot. I pretended to be really calm, took my time getting ready. I aimed extra carefully. The ball curved up in the air and—*zing!*— right over the branch.

DeVonn cheered.

I shrugged my shoulders like it was no big deal. "Let's let them go first," I said.

"I'll start." Mike made a big show of twirling the ball on his fingers. Then he shot, scored two, and missed.

DeVonn went next, scored three.

Then it was the strange kid's turn. He acted so nervous, you could tell he'd miss. And he did. Mike groaned, real loud.

When my turn came, the sun shone in my eyes, I had to squint. But that didn't matter. I started feeling great. Like the ball and I had a special deal going and my arms were made for only one thing—to zing it in over the branch. And I did exactly that, three times in a row!

"Way to go!" shouted DeVonn. He was amazed.

So was I—so amazed, I kept expecting to wake up any second in my bed, rubbing my eyes and sorry I'd only dreamed it.

But then a window banged open on the second floor of the brownstone where my stoop was. Mr. Fliegler stuck out his head. He's a bald guy with a big black mustache and a mean temper.

"Quit that racket! Knock it off, you kids!" he yelled. He slammed down the window. That was more like reality, so I knew I was awake.

"What he will do?" asked the strange kid, looking scared.

I said, "Nothing. He's just a grouch. He always yells like that."

"Forget it. Just try to throw the ball," said Mike.

We played some more. After a while, the window banged open again. Mr. Fliegler yelled even louder.

"What do I have to do to get some peace and

quiet around here? Call the police?"

The strange kid's face turned white as his shirt. "Oh, Boodgie," he said, or something like that in this low, end-of-the-world kind of voice. "Police have guns, shoot." Then he ran for all he was worth.

"Hey, it's okay. Nothing'll happen," I shouted. "Come on back!" But he raced around the corner and was gone.

"Maybe he has to catch a flying saucer," Mike kidded.

"Uh-huh. To take him back to his spaceship," said DeVonn.

I said, "Well, at least we've learned one thing—"

"Yeah? What?" asked Mike.

"They don't use tree branches for baskets much in outer space," I joked.

I hoped they'd laugh. They did. So I laughed along. I wanted to stay in good with them.

"That weirdo just didn't get it," Mike groaned. "Some teammate!"

"He sure didn't," I agreed. But I really didn't care. I just hoped he'd come around again so I could get another chance to play.

3 I'D HATE TO BE IN HIS SHOES

"WHEE-OOO!" Mike whistled through his teeth. "That is one strange kid."

"Yeah, and he's chicken, too," DeVonn said. "What did he think, a cop was going to come put him in jail?"

They plunked themselves down on my step.

I sat down, too. I felt like I was the host. I asked them, "Did you see that thing around his neck?"

"No, what was it?"

"Well, he had this shoelace with something hanging from it—"

"His door key? I used to wear mine like that," DeVonn said.

"No, something smaller. I didn't get a good look at it. But it was shiny. Know what I think?"

"What?" They were both really curious, waiting for me to tell them.

"Well, I can't say for sure. But it could have been a locket. *You* know, like girls wear." I waited for them to start laughing.

They did. So then I did, too. It felt good. I mean, the three of us laughing together.

Then DeVonn said, "Hey, what time is it?"

I checked the digital watch I got for my birthday. "Quarter to five."

"I better get home," DeVonn said.

Mike said, "Me, too."

Mike lives on Emerson Street. DeVonn lives on Dooley Avenue. I live on Palmer Place, in the other direction. But I was in no hurry, so I walked with them partway.

Mike stopped in at Izzy's, the newspaper and candy store on the corner of Emerson and Dooley. He bought a pack of MegaBubble, his favorite. "Want a piece, DeVonn? You, Shrimp?"

"Thanks." I hate grape flavor. But I started chewing anyway. And I said, "Mm!" like I liked it.

We walked across Emerson. We blew big purple bubbles and popped them really loud. I felt terrific.

Just before we came to DeVonn's, Mike said, "Hey, DeVonn, let's meet by the tree for one-on-one after school tomorrow." Like I wasn't even there. If I'd been blowing a bubble right then, it would have burst, *splat*, all over my face.

I spit out the gum.

"So long, guys."

Nobody answered. I turned my back and walked away.

I went home and let myself in.

"Dad?" I called.

He's a computer programmer and his boss is letting him work at home for as long as Mom's in Florida with Great-aunt Angie. But he didn't answer. So where was he?

It was so quiet in our apartment that my footsteps sounded extra loud. Dad's computer and the light in the kitchen were on. I knew he'd be back soon. But still, I got this empty feeling. It was like I was homesick, even though I was home.

In about ten minutes, Dad came back with big bags from the market.

"Hi, Sport." He likes to call me that. Okay with me, except it sounds too much like "short."

He lined up a bunch of stuff on the counter—onions, garlic, sausages, peppers, a box of spaghetti, a jar of tomato sauce. And he said in an extra jolly voice, "We're going to fix us *some* dinner, right?"

"Right." But a sinking feeling in my stomach said, "Wrong!" We'd been fixing ourselves "*some* dinners" the whole week. And none turned out too great.

He started chopping up onions and peppers. He used a way-too-big knife. The pieces scooted all over the cutting board.

"Let me try," I said.

But he wanted me to squeeze garlic through a garlic press. Okay, I did that.

We fried the sausages. We dumped the sauce into a big pot with all the other stuff and let it cook.

Meantime, the water for the spaghetti started boiling. So we threw in the spaghetti.

The sauce started smelling pretty good.

"One more minute," said Dad.

He rummaged in the drawer where Mom keeps ladles and things. He found a big spoon with holes in it.

He tried to fish out spaghetti to put on our plates. But he couldn't. The spaghetti was all stuck together in one great big lump.

Dad said a not-too-bad swear word in Italian. He took a sharp fork with a long handle and started hacking away at the spaghetti clump.

Just then the phone rang. I picked it up. It could have been anybody, but I said, "Mom?" because she has a way of calling right when you really want her to.

It *was* Mom. But Dad grabbed the phone away. "Listen, Marina, I'm battling this giant glob of spaghetti. It's stuck together like cement. Should I heave it in the garbage and start over, or what?"

Then he listened and said, "Sounds like a good idea. I'll give it a try." He handed me the phone.

"Mom, how's Great-aunt Angie doing?" To be honest, I didn't really care that much. I only met Great-aunt Angie one time when I was little, and I hardly even remember her. I just asked because I wanted to know when Mom was coming home.

Mom said, "She's coming along, but she still needs me."

I wanted to say, "Me, too!" But I didn't want to sound that babyish. So instead I told her about playing two-on-two with Mike and DeVonn. "And, Mom, guess who won—our team, DeVonn and me!"

"That's wonderful, Filomeno. Tell me, who else played?"

"This kid. I don't know his name. . . ." I squirmed. A picture came into my mind: Mom's face all sad and disappointed. Like when I did something she doesn't like. I didn't want to say any more. I was even glad when Dad took back the phone.

"It worked!" he told Mom, all happy. He'd put the spaghetti in a big sieve in the sink and let water run over it. "Thanks. You saved our dinner. Now we'd better eat it while it's hot. Call you later." He made a kissing noise into the phone and hung up.

Dad made me go to bed at eight because the next day was school. But I'd stayed up till eight-thirty or even nine that whole week and gotten used to it. I couldn't fall asleep for the longest time. I just wasn't tired.

Besides, I kept seeing that kid in my mind: How he looked so out of it and couldn't say things right. How he got so scared, like it was the end of the world, when Mr. Fliegler yelled at us about making too much noise.

I thought, I'm glad I'm not that kid. I'd hate to be in his shoes. And I punched my pillow. Then I fluffed it. But it wasn't the pillow's fault. I just couldn't get comfortable.

I had to face it: I only got to play because that kid showed up. He did me a favor and what did *I* do? Crack jokes about him. Maybe that's what bothered me.

4 SLOB-O

"SPACE PATROLS ARE planning to capture this school!" Mike told DeVonn when we got to our classroom Monday morning.

DeVonn laughed. "That would be cool. Who told you? The guy with the pointy ears from *Star Trek*?"

"No. But guess who I ran into?"

DeVonn drew a blank.

I put in my two cents, "That weirdo kid from yesterday?"

"That's the one," said Mike. "He kept asking, 'Where iss office?' And he was standing right in front of it! He was acting like he was lost. But maybe he was taking photos with a secret robot camera and transmitting information to his space buddies—"

"Hey, look!" DeVonn pointed to the door.

The kid walked in. He was wearing those same pants, a grown-up shirt too big on him, even a tie. His hair looked like it was slicked down with glue. He was kind of bent over, like he wanted to hide how tall he was.

Our teacher wasn't there yet. Kids were still hanging out—talking to the gerbils, drawing on the board, having eraser fights, stuff like that. So not everyone saw him right away when he walked in.

"This iss two-oh-three? Class of Miss Otiss?" he asked in his foreign accent.

Then kids noticed and whispered, "Huh? Who's that?"

Mike poked DeVonn on the arm and said, "What did I tell you?"

I was getting ready to answer the strange kid. But Luz Mendes beat me to it. "Are you trying to say Ms. Ortiz's class? Room 203? Yes, that's where you are."

Everybody stared at him, wondering if this much older guy was going to be in our class. And if so, how come?

"Hey, remember me?" DeVonn went over to him and pretend threw him a ball.

Mike pretend intercepted it. He said, "You're too old for this class! How old *are* you, anyway? Twelve? Thirteen? Or do they count kids' ages by billions of years where you come from?"

DeVonn and some other kids laughed.

Mike took a piece of chalk and drew a great big picture all over the chalkboard. He made a weird thing, like a flying saucer. He put clouds all over the place. Then he took Ms. Ortiz's pointer and pointed above the clouds. "That's outer space up there," he said. "Is that where you came from?"

The kid looked blank. "I no understand."

So then Mike drew a line near the bottom. "That's

Earth." He drew a stick figure with big baggy pants standing on the line. He labeled it, Kid from Outer Space. Then he poked the kid hard in the chest and said, "That's you."

Everybody laughed and started shooting questions at him: "Where *do* you come from?"

"What's your name?"

"What language do you speak?"

The kid looked scared and confused. He didn't answer.

By then it was almost nine-fifteen. Kids started to sit down.

"Where I sit?" the strange kid asked.

Steve Weinglass said, "Wait. Ms. Ortiz will show you. She'll be here soon."

"No, don't wait," said Mike. "*I'll* show you. Sit right there." He pointed to the teacher's desk.

"That not belong to teacher?" the kid asked.

Mike copied his accent, "Yes, it belong to teacher. But—" He looked around the room, signaling that kids shouldn't laugh or even grin, but should play along with his joke.

"New kids get to sit there on their first day. Honest, I wouldn't fool you." He pushed the strange kid over to Ms. Ortiz's desk. "Come on, sit down, it's okay."

I'm an expert on getting laughed at. I was all set to warn him, "No, it's not okay, don't sit there!" But I

wanted to see what would happen. I mean, here was my chance to watch somebody else be the joke.

But even without my warning, the kid did not sit down. He just stood there. So the whole thing fizzled out.

Then Ms. Ortiz ran in.

I always feel good when I see her. She's the kind of teacher everybody wants. She makes things fun, even homework. She never picks on anybody. And she almost never yells.

"Sorry I'm late. My bus hit a taxi, everyone had to get off—" Then she saw the strange kid standing by her desk and gave him a big smile.

He handed her a note from the office.

When she was done reading it, she turned around and saw the flying saucer and stuff on the board.

She shook her head like she was upset. She looked around the room. "What's been going on here? To what budding young Picasso do we owe this work of art?"

Everybody kept quiet. Out on the street a car alarm and squeaking truck brakes sounded extra loud.

Ms. Ortiz shrugged her shoulders. "Well, all right. I can see why the artist would rather not take credit." She grabbed an eraser and wiped the whole board clean.

She put her hand on the strange kid's shoulder. "Class, let me explain a few things. This boy is older than you and should be in a higher grade. But the most important thing for him to do right now is to learn English. And he can do that more easily in this class. I hope you'll help him all you can. His name is . . ."

She studied the note. "Now let me get this right." She took chalk and started to spell it out on the board. S-L-O-B-O

Kids started giggling.

Ms. Ortiz spun around. "I don't need eyes in the back of my head. I can hear *exactly* who's laughing. Dave Behar, Mike Donnelly, Molly Satz, and anyone else who can't control yourself, see me after school."

She finished spelling out the strange kid's name. S-L-O-B-O-D-A-N V-L-A-D-I-Č. She put a little mark over the C and said that makes it sound like "tch."

She turned to him. "Can you pronounce it for us? Please, don't be shy. Say it loud and clear."

His face went red as tomatoes. "Slob-o—," he said, hardly above a whisper. Kids sucked in their breath and chewed their lips so they wouldn't bust out laughing. "Slob-o-dan—"

"I see nothing funny," said Ms. Ortiz. "Now your last name. How do you say it? Vla-ditz?"

He shook his head. "Vla-*ditch*."

"As in *rich*, *witch*, and—"

"Mike Donnelly, kindly spare us your rhymes." Ms. Ortiz can sound more disgusted with her voice low than other teachers can when they're yelling their throats sore.

"Now, Slobodan, please tell the class where you come from."

He cleared his throat. "Split," he said.

Dave, Mike, and Molly laughed out loud. I guess they figured why not, since they already had to see Ms. Ortiz after school.

DeVonn folded a piece of paper and passed it.

I usually don't get notes passed to me. I mean, I never did before. But this one came to me!

It said, "*Split*, like in split your sides. Ha-ha!"

When I read it to myself, I did just about split my sides. I couldn't help it.

Ms. Ortiz's eyes are really dark, almost black. She looked at me like there was fire in them. She was really, really mad.

"Slobodan, please excuse this rudeness." And she asked, "Now, does anyone here know where Split might be?"

Nobody knew.

She drew a curved shape with bumps on it on the board. "This is a rough outline of an area in Europe. It used to be a country called Yugoslavia. Now it's broken up into several parts that want to be separate countries." She drew another bumpy line around one part. "This part is called Croatia (crow-AY-sha). Slobodan comes from there. Slobodan, can you show us where Split is?"

She handed him the chalk. He made a mark on the map. "This here is Split."

"Thank you, Slobodan. Now you may sit down."
She pointed to an empty seat two tables away from
mine.

Later, when everyone was running out to recess, Ms.
Ortiz called me up to her desk. She held her hand
out, "Give it."

I knew what she meant, but I tried to look blank.

"The note," she said.

I handed it over. I had to.

"Very funny." She gave me a sarcastic look. Then
she asked the question teachers always ask, even the
nice ones, "Who sent it?"

I looked down at her shiny brown shoes and said,
"I'd rather not tell, Ms. Ortiz."

"No, of course not." Then she let me go to recess.

5 SUPER MEAT LOAF?

"DID SHE ASK who sent the note?" DeVonn asked as soon as I hit the playground.

"Mm-hm."

"Did you tell?"

"No way."

"Hey, thanks. You did good!"

"DeVonn, get back here," Mike yelled. They were in the middle of playing wall ball. Wall ball is a lot like handball, except you're allowed more bounces.

DeVonn asked, "Shrimp, you want to play?"

"Sure!"

Meantime, Charlie Cardozo was playing, too.

Mike said, "Four's too many."

"Says who? Shrimp's in or else I'm out," DeVonn said. "Which is it?"

So Mike said, "Okay, okay."

And it was fun.

The one not having too much fun that recess, or the next, or the next, was the kid from Split.

Naturally everyone called him Slob-o. Me included. Even though I knew how it felt when kids called you dumb, stupid names. But he didn't even know what a slob was. So, what the heck, why not?

Nobody wanted Slob-o on teams or in games because they always had to explain everything first. And since he didn't know much English, it took him a long time to catch on.

So kids hardly even talked to him. Except to tease him. "How are you doing with English? Learned any new words lately?"

He'd say, "Wall ball, homework, spelling quiz." And kids would start laughing and imitating his accent, before he even turned his back.

DeVonn invited me to come over after school on Wednesday.

I went home first to tell Dad. He looked disappointed. That reminded me.

"Oh, right, we were going to the computer store." Dad wanted to check out laptops. He's thinking of buying a new one. When he does, *if* he does, I get to use his old one.

Dad said, "That's okay. We'll go some other time. Go on to DeVonn's. Have fun."

When I got there, DeVonn and Mike were out on the sidewalk shooting bottle caps.

I didn't have any on me, so I just stood around and watched.

Then I said, "Guess who I see!"

It was Slob-o, coming out of Washabee's, the Laundromat across the street. He carried a bunch of laundry. He was wearing a T-shirt, not the dress-up kind of shirt and tie he wore to school. And he had his usual gloomy look, like there's no such thing as fun in the whole wide world.

"Hey, Slob-o, come over here!" I called.

First thing he did when he saw us was grab the thing on the string around his neck and stick it inside his shirt. Then he came over.

Mike and DeVonn said, "Hi, Slob-o. How ya doing?"

He cleared his throat and pointed to his shirt. "Shirt clean, no dirt." Then to his shoes. "Shoes polished." Then to his head. "Hair combed." And he said, looking very serious, "I no am slob!"

Mike laughed.

DeVonn said, "Hey, you finally learned what 'slob' means." And he asked, "What other new words did you learn?"

"Bottle caps." He pointed to them.

"Good! What else?"

"Fluff dry. Det-ergent." Only he put the accent on "det," so it sounded pretty weird. "Thank you for not smoking. Hey, you guys. Have nice day."

"That's good. You have nice day, too," I said.

"Is that all?" asked Mike.

"No. I also learn turnstile, like is in subway.

Express. Local. Sportscaster on TV. Long-distance operator. Watch out, wet paint." He reeled off all those words.

"You're doing good," DeVonn said.

"Wait. I not yet finished. Franks, french fries, meat loaf, super."

"Super meat loaf?" Mike rubbed his stomach. "Mm, yum."

Slob-o didn't like that. "No, not super meat loaf!"

"Super what then?" I asked.

"Super you?" DeVonn pointed at him. "Like, you think you're pretty great?"

Slob-o shook his head. "No." Then he said, "Poppa."

"Popper? What kind of popper?" asked Mike.

DeVonn asked, "Poppa, like a dad?"

Slob-o nodded.

"Your dad? Your dad is great? Is that what you're trying to say?" Mike and DeVonn were laughing. "What's so great about him?"

Slob-o got insulted. "You no understand. See you, guys." He walked away.

DeVonn and I shook our heads, like trying to talk with him was hopeless.

"I have a great idea," said Mike. "Let's be private eyes. *You* know, detectives. Let's go solve the mystery of exactly what's so super. Shh, we have to be real quiet! Follow me!"

We followed Mike, who followed Slob-o down the

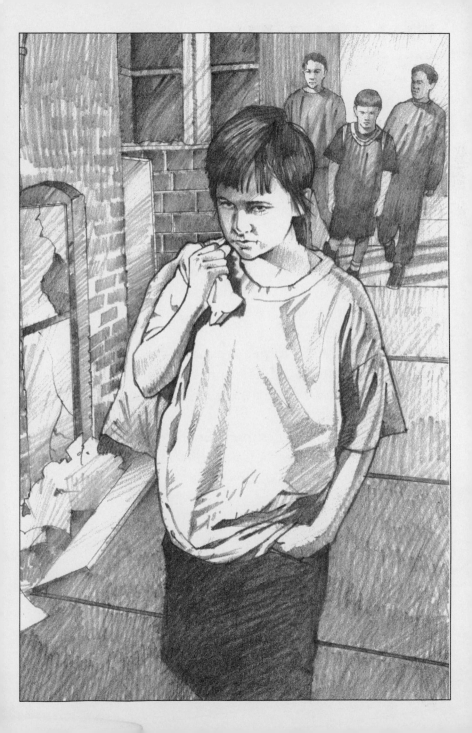

block. We stayed pretty far behind. When we got to the corner, we speeded up to see which way he'd turn.

He turned onto Cargill. We did, too. That's not a street my dad would be thrilled to see me walking on. It's kind of ratty, with bars, an offtrack betting parlor, and buildings with smashed-in windows.

I was glad when Slob-o hung a left at the corner and turned onto Meadows. But then he stopped and just stood still right in the middle of the block.

Was he lost or what? We ducked into a doorway and watched.

All of a sudden he turned around and pointed to us.

"Hey, you guys!" And he grinned, like he knew right along that we were following him. He signaled us to come closer.

We did. I felt pretty embarrassed.

"You walk with me," he said. Like he really wanted us to. "I show you where I live."

SLOB-O'S POPPA

MIKE AND DEVONN walked on either side of Slob-o. They looked like three pals out for a stroll.

I trailed along behind. I wished I'd gone to the computer store. Then I wouldn't be doing this.

We walked down Meadows Street for a block and a half. For a street that once upon a time was meadows, it was not too pretty. A homeless woman slept in a doorway. Lots of stuff you wouldn't want to say out loud was written on the walls.

Halfway down the block, a man stuffed trash bags into garbage cans in front of a gray four-story building. He still had one trash bag left in his hand. But then he saw us coming. He got all happy and came toward us, still holding the trash bag.

He looked a lot like Slob-o, only grown up. He had the same green eyes, same brown hair. It even fell into his face the same way.

He gave us this big, wide smile.

"Hello! You friends of my boy, yes?"

We said, "Hi."

Slob-o told him our names.

His poppa shook our hands.

"So nice of you that you come for visit."

He went on ahead to the house with the garbage cans out front. He stuffed the trash bag he'd been carrying into a can. Then he made sure all the lids were on tight.

"Before, things here not so clean. Garbage on sidewalk, in hall inside building." He held his nose. "Bad smell. But now, whole building—how you say—spic, span? My son, he help. We do A-OK, good job."

We went inside.

The hall did not smell bad. But it sure was dark.

We went to the end of the hall, to Apartment 1W. A sign under the peephole in the door said, Milovan Vladič, Superintendent.

Mr. Vladič unlocked the door. He put his hand on his waist and he bowed. Like he was a baron or a count or somebody like that. "Now please, you come in."

It was almost as dark in their apartment as outside in the hall.

He showed us around. "This front room is living room and bedroom. This couch, I sleep. This room nice, even has sunshine."

A tiny sliver of sun came through the window. That and some posters were the only cheerful things in the room. One poster was of a town with little white houses up on a hill. Another showed a sailboat on the sea. They both had foreign writing on them.

There was a bookcase with big, heavy, foreign books. But no curtains or rugs. And only one sick-looking plant with hardly any leaves on the windowsill.

"Now, here is bathroom. And this is room of Slobodan."

Slob-o's room was very neat, with not much in it. Outside his window was a dark gray wall that made the room feel like a jail.

"And here is kitchen."

Their kitchen was one hundred percent different from mine. I don't mean because the refrigerator looked like it was from when refrigerators were first invented or because there was no dishwasher. I mean because there weren't things like pot holders. No spice rack, either. No spoons with holes, no strainer hanging near the stove. No place for cookbooks. No fancy magnets on the refrigerator door holding recipes or pictures. It did not seem like a place where cooking or eating meals was fun.

Mr. Vladič carried in two more chairs—one from the front room and one from Slob-o's room. And a step stool.

He said, "Now you please sit down."

He brought out pretzels, marshmallow cookies, and raisin cookies.

"You like chocolate sodas?" he asked us and took down five glasses. He put in gobs of chocolate syrup. Then soda water. He gave us spoons. "Now stir it,

good. You know what long ago people call this drink?"

We shook our heads.

"Egg cream. No egg, no cream, but that was name. Old man in candy store told to me. Funny, yes?"

Yes. We laughed politely.

Mr. Vladič raised his glass. "I drink to health of friends of Slobodan!"

"Poppa, wait." Slob-o said something in their language. Maybe that the three of us really only came here as a joke and weren't his friends at all . . .

I got ready for Mr. Vladič to grab us by our collars and shove us out the door.

"I make mistake," he said, still with his smile on. "I forget, egg cream not good without milk," he said. He poured some into everybody's glass and stirred. "Now drink. I hope you like. This is very special occasion. First time my boy have visit of friends. I thank that you come."

The egg cream tasted good. But a big swallow of it went down the wrong way. I started coughing and I coughed up a storm.

DeVonn hit me on the back. Mr. Vladič got me some water.

Then I felt okay again—but just in my throat.

The rest of me didn't feel okay.

I hated the polite smiles on our faces—Mike's, DeVonn's, and mine.

I hated that Slob-o was sitting there all quiet, and none of us could think of a single thing to say to him.

I hated how Mike and DeVonn were going to laugh it up and kid around later. I could almost hear them already. "That super was super, yeah. . . ."

The thing I hated most was lying. And I was, by sitting there letting Mr. Vladič think we were Slob-o's friends.

The only way I could think of stopping was to lie even more.

"I just remembered, I have to go someplace with my father," I said. "Thanks for the egg cream and cookies. Bye!"

And I beat it out of there.

EYE-TIE

I RAN THE whole way home.

"You're all out of breath," said Dad. "What happened? Did you and DeVonn have a fight?"

"No."

"Then how come you're back early?"

"I don't know. I just wasn't having such a good time." And I asked, "Can we still go to the computer store?"

Dad said, "I guess. If you really want to."

I didn't care that much if he got a new laptop. I could always use the one he had. But I'm glad we went because it made what I said about having to go someplace less of a lie.

The salespeople were nice to us, even after Dad decided not to buy anything. They let us try out a whole bunch of new games.

The best one was called Hexapix. It has lots of different size shapes with six sides in pink and purple and polka dots and stripes. You can stack them up and down or sideways. (Whichever way you zap them off the screen the fastest, the more points you score.)

Then there was one I didn't like, Space Eraser. It

had whole armies of space guys. The trick was to make them jump and spin around so they would wipe each other out. I didn't even want to try.

Dad said, "It looks interesting. Why not?"

"I don't know," I said. I wasn't in the mood for space guys. Or fighting.

We spent lots of time in the games department. When we finally left the store, we were starving.

"There's nothing much to eat at home," Dad said.

He ducked into a food store and bought TV dinners—one Swiss steak and one pork chops.

I don't like either of those. If they didn't have the name of the food on the package, you'd never know which was which. They both taste like cardboard, only salty, and kind of like somebody already chewed it all up but didn't swallow it down.

So I wasn't looking forward to dinner very much. But just when we got ready to pop them in the microwave, we were saved by the bell. How come she always knows just when it's the perfect time?

As usual, Dad talked first.

His end of the conversation went: "Mm-hm, mm-hm. That's good, sure. Well, I suppose you have to. Oh, just TV dinners. No, I forgot all about it!" Suddenly he sounded in a great mood. "He's fine. He's right here. I'll put him on—" About time!

"Hi, Mom!" I was so glad to hear her voice.

She said Great-aunt Angie was doing better, no

more fever, and was out of bed. But she had no appetite. And she needed food to build up her strength. So Mom had to keep encouraging her to eat.

"And to cook great meals for her," I said with a big sigh.

"Right," Mom said. "It's still too soon to leave Great-aunt Angie on her own. But I'll be home next week." As though that was really soon!

I asked, "What day next week?"

She didn't know yet. She said, "Just think how great it'll be when we're all together again. Meantime, Dad needs your company."

The next thing she said was a mystery to me: "I hope you enjoy your dinner!"

Now, Mom is not a big kidder. She doesn't rub things in. And she knew what we were having—Dad told her! So what was going on?

Dad reached into the freezer. He brought out a covered dish and said, "Ta-da! Chicken and sausages à la Marina! Mom made it for us before she left. She told me, but I forgot all about it!"

It only took six minutes to heat up. It was tomatoey, spicy, and garlicky just the way we love it.

It was dee-licious!

While we were eating, I looked around our kitchen and noticed the homey things: The blue-and-white plaid curtains blowing in the breeze. Two of Mom's African violets on the windowsill starting to bloom. The bright-colored pictures I drew in art class that Mom had put on the refrigerator.

Dad said, "It's almost like your mom is sitting right here with us." He patted her empty chair.

"Yeah." It felt that way to me, too. Then I thought of where Slob-o and his father live. How when they don't have company, there are only two chairs at their kitchen table.

After dinner, I did homework. Then we watched TV.

Shield of Honor was on. Two police detectives were trailing somebody they thought was a crook.

I said, "Dad, could we watch something else?"

"You usually like this show. Why not tonight?"

"I don't know. I just don't."

He turned off the TV. He looked me in the eyes and said, "Something's bothering you, I can tell. Did kids give you a hard time today, or what?"

"No, they didn't."

"You miss Mom. I know, I do, too."

"Yeah, but that isn't it."

"Then what is it, Son?"

"I just don't feel like talking about it."

He was going to turn the TV back on. But then I said, "Can I ask you something?"

"Shoot."

"How old were you when you came to America? What was it like?"

"Let me see. . . . . I was eleven. No, I'd just turned twelve. It was, well—" Dad leaned back on the couch and closed his eyes for a second. "It was pretty bad. You know how grown-ups sometimes say they wish they could be that age again? *I* don't. It was about the worst time in my life."

"How come?"

"We lived on my grandfather's farm in Connecticut. I didn't know anybody—"

"Could you speak English?"

"I'd learned a little in my school in Italy. But I was too shy to open my mouth. I was a laughingstock. Kids all had a great time making fun of me. You've had a taste of that yourself."

He told me all the ha-ha ways they said Pazzalini. "And you know what else they called me? Eye-tie. I still get mad when I think about it."

"What does it mean?"

"Nothing. It's short for *Eye-talian*, that's how they said it. It was insulting, that's all." He told me how lousy and lonely he'd felt.

Then he said, "You never asked me about any of that before. How come now? Are you doing family histories or something in school?"

"No. I was just curious because there's a new kid in our class. He's from a country that used to be Yugoslavia."

"Oh. Well, it's different coming to a big city. Lots

of kids in your school come from lots of different parts of the world. So this new kid doesn't stick out like a sore thumb the way I did. It's easier for him, right?"

Easier? It was true that our school had lots of kids from other countries, but probably none from the place he came from. And none who spoke with his thick weird accent. A picture came into my mind— Slob-o, tall and gangly in his dress-up shirt and baggy pants, looking lost and probably feeling like a freak. I knew *I* would if I were that big and old and got put in a grade with younger, shorter kids.

No, he didn't have it easier. He stuck out just as bad or even worse. And he was probably homesick, too. I knew *I* would be, if I suddenly had to move to a new country that was thousands of miles away.

8 MAKE-BELIEVE BASKETBALL BRAWL

FRIDAY, WHEN SCHOOL let out, I heard Mike talking to DeVonn and Charlie Cardozo.

"Meet me tomorrow by the tree. Ten o'clock, if it's nice out. Be there," Mike told them.

They said, "Okay."

I was standing right there waiting for them to ask me. But they didn't. So I said, "Can I come?"

DeVonn said, "Yeah, we'll need a fourth."

"Sorry," said Mike. "I already asked Lorenzo Mendes. He's really good."

When I got home, Dad said, "Something wrong, Sport?"

I said, "Oh, nothing . . ."

"Hm." Dad scrunched his eyes shut and touched his hands to the sides of his head, like he was getting brain waves. This was his magic-mind-reader act. "Something *is* wrong. Now, let me see. . . . Could it be about Sycamore Street? Shooting make-believe baskets?"

"No, it's about *not* shooting them. Those guys never want me to play—"

"We'll soon fix that," Dad said. "Just give me a couple of minutes."

His fingers zipped around on the keyboard, *clacketa, clack*. "There. Done for today." He exited the program and switched off his computer.

"Okay, now get your jacket. Bring your ball. You're about to turn into the most wanted player in this entire neighborhood."

Dad put on his basketball shoes, and we left.

I thought we were going to Sycamore Street to practice by the tree.

"That's kid stuff," Dad said. "Stick with me."

We went to the real basketball courts in the park by the river, where I'm never allowed except with a grown-up.

Dad gave me a real workout. First I thought, This is impossible, because the hoops were so high and I'm so short. I couldn't even throw the ball that high, much less dunk it in. But Dad kept saying, "You're doing okay, just keep at it." I must have thrown that ball about a million times. Finally, *finally*, it went in. And pretty soon I did it again!

"Okay, now let's have some fun," Dad said. So we played one-on-one. He's not the kind of grown-up who holds back and misses shots on purpose. He played his best. Naturally, he won.

"But not by that much," he said, clapping me on

the back. "You did great. Those guys on Sycamore Street are in for a big surprise!"

Yeah. Except, they were already four. There was still my same old problem, being odd kid out.

"If you want something really bad, go for it!" somebody said in a book I read, I don't remember which. Anyway, when Dad and I got home from the park, I looked up Vladič in the phone book. And I called.

"Oh, Shrimp? I remember. You come visit," said Mr. Vladič. He was glad to hear from me. "Slobodan not home. Yes, I will give him message about basketball, for sure."

On Saturday morning, the sun was shining. All the birds that live in holes in the walls of buildings were whistling and singing like it was going to be a great day. I put on the Dolphins shirt Mom sent me from Florida and headed for Sycamore Street.

I was the first one there. I sat down and waited. If worse came to worse and Slob-o didn't show, well, I'd just make more of an imprint on my step from sitting there watching, like all the other times.

But he came, right on the dot at ten. He didn't even look that weird. His pants weren't so baggy and he had on a regular T-shirt. But he still kind of stared down at the ground, like he was afraid to say hi or anything.

Mike, DeVonn, Charlie, and Lorenzo all arrived together. They started arguing about who should play on whose team.

I asked them in a bored voice, like it was all the same to me, "Hey, guys, how about playing three against three?"

"With you and *him*? No, thanks," said Mike.

"Aw, be human," said DeVonn. "Give them a break."

"Yeah, why not?" said Lorenzo. "Three against three is more fun."

So they changed the teams: Mike, Charlie, and me against DeVonn, Lorenzo, and Slob-o.

I thought, Wait till they see how good I got! Then I missed my first two shots. Oh, well.

Then it was Slob-o's turn. He acted less nervous. Bingo, his first shot sailed right over the branch.

"Wuh-oh, it's Magic Vladič!" Mike laughed. "Just don't get too cocky, 'cause no way will you do that again. No *way*!" He started jumping up and down, circling his arms like chopper blades right in Slob-o's face, and yelling, "Drop it, drop it!"

After a while, Slob-o did. Anybody would have. And quick, he stooped down for the ball.

Mike did, too, and tried to push him away.

I was standing right there. I saw every move.

Slob-o pushed Mike back and made a grab for the ball. Mike grabbed for something, too. Only it wasn't the ball. It was the shoelace Slob-o wore around his neck. That thing he always kept hidden inside his shirt.

Mike yanked it out. For a second I saw what was hanging from it.

"Hey, guess what," Mike shouted. "This guy is wearing a locket! Take it off! Come on, show us your locket, Slob-o!"

Slob-o made a noise in his throat like a growl. He clutched onto the shoelace and tugged for all he was worth, trying to make Mike let go.

The shoelace tore. The locket fell off.

Slob-o let out a groan and put his hands over his face.

Mike swooped down. So did Slob-o. So did I.

We scrambled around on the pavement. Mike had the locket. Slob-o tried to claw his fingers loose. So did I. We couldn't do it.

Then I remembered a trick—twisting somebody's wrist in two directions, using both your hands. And I tried it, really hard.

"Ouch, that hurts!" Mike yelled. He hauled out with his other hand and punched me. I think he meant to hit me on the arm. Instead, he caught me in the nose. It didn't hurt that much. But when I touched my hand to it, my fingers turned red. Blood dripped down all over my Dolphins shirt.

9 BLOODY NOSE

"SHRIMP'S HURT! He's bleeding all over the place!"

Everybody crowded around me except Slob-o. Mike was the most upset. He even apologized.

"Hey, I'm sorry. I didn't mean to hit you that hard." And he gave me his handkerchief.

"My mom's home. Should I get her?" asked DeVonn.

Lorenzo lives right on that block. He said, "No, I'll get my mom. She's a nurse. She'll know what to do. Want me to?"

I said, "No, thanks. I'll be okay. It's only a nosebleed."

They made me sit down. They told me, "Hold your head back. No, hold it down. Squeeze your nose shut."

I held my head down and squeezed my nose shut—with just one hand, my left.

They asked me a couple of times, "Is it stopping?"

"Almost."

"Are you okay?"

"Sure."

"All right. Then come on, guys, let's play," said Mike. He, DeVonn, Charlie, and Lorenzo headed back to the tree.

All this time, Slob-o was standing by himself over by the next stoop. Now he walked over to Mike. He stuck out his hand and said in a growly voice, "You no play yet. First you give to me—"

Mike shoved his hand away. "Give you what?" he asked, sounding really mad.

"*You* know what. Give back to me, right now."

"I no have it, Slob-o. Let me by." Mike shoved him out of the way and ran.

Charlie was dribbling the ball. Mike grabbed it and ran with it. "*I* get first turn!"

I guess I moved my head too much, watching. Or I let up on holding my nose shut. Anyway, it started bleeding again.

Slob-o came over to my stoop. "Much blood on handkerchief," he said. "Handkerchief no good now." He took a bunch of tissues out of his pants pocket. "Here, I give you."

"Thanks."

I took the tissues. I held one to my nose and squeezed my nose shut extra tight—still with just one hand.

Slob-o looked miserable.

He started to ask, "You have my . . ."

Yes, I had it. Twisting Mike's wrist two ways had done the trick. Mike had to open his fist for a second, long enough for me to grab the locket. I'd been

clutching it in my right hand all this time.

"Here." I gave it back.

He took a great big breath. I never saw anybody look so relieved. His eyes looked like all that relief was going to spill over. I turned away in case it did. I figured he didn't need somebody watching him cry.

My nose felt okay. I didn't think it would start to bleed again, so I stood up. I moved down to the first step of the stoop. That way he and I could stand face-to-face.

"Hey, Sl—" Suddenly that name, Slob-o, stuck in my throat. I didn't want to say it to his face. So I didn't call him anything. I just said, "Thanks for the tissues."

"You welcome. Thanks for giving me back my— how you say?"

"Locket. You're welcome, too. Can I ask you something?"

"Yes, ask."

"What's in it? Would you show me?"

He was holding it so tight, I could see the knuckles of his hand turn white. "First *I* ask *you* something."

"What?"

"Boy have locket, you no think it funny?"

Hm. I needed to think about that.

The locket was silver with a flower design on it. I never saw a boy wear a locket like that. *I* sure wouldn't. Kids would definitely laugh their heads off if a boy wore a locket like that.

It made me think of when I was the prince in the Valentine's Day play back in first grade. My mom made me a heart out of silver foil to wear around my neck. She thought it would go great with my costume. So I wore it. But I felt funny about it. And sure enough, when I got to our classroom, everybody started giggling and making fun of me. So I took it off in a hurry and threw it away.

Anyway, all the guys I know would definitely laugh their heads off about a boy wearing a locket. *I* did, the day we first noticed it. Would I again if I was with a bunch of them?

I'd want to be one of the gang. So, yeah, I would probably laugh. But did that mean that personally and privately I thought it was funny?

That was the big question. I took my time. I thought about it from every angle. Then I gave my honest answer, "No. Other guys would. But I don't think it's funny.

"You are sure?"

"Absolutely, positively, one hundred percent."

He believed me. And he said, "Okay. I show you."

The locket was only about the size of a quarter. I watched his fingers working as he opened it. His fingernails *were* really clean. I thought, It's true what he said the other day. This guy is definitely not a slob. Slob-o—what a dumb, stupid name!

I'm through with that name, I decided.

Slobodan—"Slow-bow-dan"—I practiced saying it. It *was* long and hard to say, but so what?

THE LOCKET

INSIDE THE LOCKET was a curl of dark brown hair and a face cut out of a photo. The face had a mom kind of smile on it.

So I asked, "Is it your mother?"

"Yes." He snapped the locket shut and clenched his fist over it. Then his shoulders shook, like he was cold or something. And the thing happened that didn't happen before, when I gave him back the locket. A great big sob ripped out of him. He started to cry. Not just one or two tears. A whole flood.

The last thing a guy who's crying needs is somebody watching. So I looked away, like to check out if any boats were floating by on the river. When I turned back around, he was running up the street as fast as if he had on RollerBlades.

He wasn't watching where he was going. When he got near the corner of Emerson Street, he ran smack into somebody walking the other way. It was my dad! Oh, boy.

My dad didn't even care that Slobodan nearly knocked him over because then he caught sight of me. He started running like *he* had blades on, pushing right through the basketball game, yelling, "What happened? Are you okay?"

"Yeah, I'm okay. I just got a nosebleed, that's all."

"Is it still bleeding?"

"No, it stopped."

Dad took out his handkerchief and wiped at my nose to make sure. "Did you get hurt anyplace else?"

"No, I'm fine. Really!"

So then Dad quit worrying. "And here I thought I'd get to watch my kid playing like a champ," he said, all disappointed. Like all the work he put in yesterday trying to sharpen me up was for nothing.

"Dad, I *did* play. Not too bad, either. But then there was a fight—"

"What about?"

"It's hard to explain—"

"And somebody punched you, right?"

"Yeah."

"Did you punch him back?"

"I didn't get a chance."

Just then, *swish* and *swish*, Charlie sank two balls in a row, really fast.

"Yay, we're winning!" Lorenzo cheered.

"Not yet you aren't!" DeVonn captured the ball and got ready to shoot.

Dad put his hand on my shoulder. "Well, it doesn't look as though you'll get to play anymore today. So what do you say we go home and clean you up?"

*   *   *

We put my Dolphins shirt in the sink to soak.

I took a good long shower.

Then Dad wanted to hear about the kid who bumped into him and what the fight was about.

"He's the new kid in our class I told you about, remember?"

"Right. From what used to be Yugoslavia. He looks a lot older than you. Like he should be in fifth grade or even sixth."

"Yeah, but he hardly knows any English. That's why they put him with us."

Dad asked, "Was the fight about him?"

"Yeah, sort of."

"How do you mean, sort of?" We were sitting on the couch where we watch TV. Dad put both hands on my shoulders and looked me square in the face. For a couple of seconds it was like our eyes were having a conversation.

Then Dad ruffled my hair and said, "You'd just as soon not go into it, right?"

"Yeah." Especially not the locket part. I didn't know why exactly, but I really didn't want to tell about that.

Dad turned on the TV news. The first thing was about stuff happening in Sarajevo, in Bosnia. They showed a bomb exploding. A house with its roof torn off. People who got hurt lying on a sidewalk, all bloody.

I asked, "Dad, is that near Split?"

"Well," said Dad, "it's not that big an area, so it's probably pretty near."

In my mind I saw the hair and face inside the locket and how Slobodan looked when he snapped it shut. I got a scary feeling in my stomach.

"Dad?"

"What is it?"

"When's Mom coming home?"

Dad said, "Either Tuesday or Wednesday."

Three more days. Or even four!

The Vladičs' kitchen came into my mind. I could see those chairs at their table. . . . Only two!

When the commercial came on, I told Dad about Slobodan's locket. What was inside. And I said, "I wonder where his mom is."

"You could call him up and ask him," Dad said.

"Uh-uh. He'll think it's none of my business. Besides, what if she's—you know?"

Dad rubbed his bald spot. "Yeah. Well. But you could still call him."

"What for?"

"Just to be friendly."

"What would I say?"

Dad rubs that spot on top of his head when he's thinking. And he came up with an idea. He said, "You and I deserve a break from our own cooking, don't you think? So why don't you invite him to come have dinner with us at Luigi's?"

I went to the phone. I still had the Vladičs' number from yesterday. And I called.

"Hello, Mr. Vladič? It's Shrimp. Can I talk to Slobodan?"

"Just a moment."

But then Mr. Vladič got back on the phone and said, "Slobodan not want to talk."

"Why not?"

"He ashamed," Mr. Vladič said.

I swallowed like something was stuck in my throat. I didn't know what to say.

"What you want I tell him?" Mr. Vladič asked.

"Tell him my dad is inviting him for dinner at Luigi's Restaurant. They have Italian food there. It's really good."

Mr. Vladič went and talked to him in their language.

Then Slobodan came to the phone. And he said yes.

11 THE OCTOPUS

LUIGI'S HAS DELICIOUS food. Also, there's a cool-looking octopus with curly arms on the ceiling right over where you eat. Still, I was pretty nervous.

We rang the bell. Slobodan came to the door looking all spruced up for the occasion. His hair was slicked down, and he wore a white shirt and tie.

Was he wearing the locket? I couldn't tell. But I hoped so. I don't know why. I just did.

"Hi, this is my dad," I said. "Dad, this is Slobodan Vladič." I think I said his name right.

Then Slobodan's father came out of the kitchen. I introduced him to my dad.

"So kind, you invite my boy to restaurant," said Mr. Vladič.

Dad said, "It's our pleasure. Why don't you come, too?"

Mr. Vladič smiled and shook his head. "I stay here. Much work to do. But I appreciate, very much."

He and Dad shook hands and we left for Luigi's.

Luigi, the owner, put us at the table right near the octopus.

Slobodan went over to it. He touched it. He put

his finger in one of the suckers on its arms, like to see if it would grab. Of course it didn't. It was only plastic. But it did something I hadn't been able to do and neither had my dad. It made Slobodan smile, like seeing that octopus actually made him feel good.

He sure liked the salami, anchovies, olives, pimientos, and peppers in the antipasto, too. He finished up his share so fast that Dad ordered a whole other one.

All the way over here, Dad and I were trying to think of things to talk about that would interest Slobodan. But he'd mostly just said yes and no.

Now he started talking. "Once I saw swimming, a real one—" He pointed to the wall. "How you say?"

"Octopus. Where?" I asked.

"In sea. We were in a boat on sea. Octopus came swimming near. I could almost touch. Other boat came. It belong to fisherman. Fisherman catched octopus. Its arms did this—" He waved his arms in the air. "Was angry to be catched. But octopus meat good to eat. My mother cook for supper, many times."

Dad asked, "Where were you living?"

"In Split." Slobodan told us that one part of the town was on top of a hill with small white houses. It was very old. And the new part was down on the beach with stores and hotels. "It was beautiful place," he said.

"When did you come to America?" Dad asked. "How did you come here?"

"On second of April. In airplane. By myself. My father here already. He meet me at airport."

Dad asked the question that was on both our minds. "And your mother?"

Slobodan's eyes went dark and sad, like when he showed me the locket.

The waiter came with our main courses. He put our plates down in front of us and was all cheerful. He wished us *"buon appetito,"* Italian for "good appetite."

I thought, We might not have any appetite. We might not eat a single bite. It all depended on what Slobodan would say.

Finally the waiter was done, and Slobodan answered the question. "My mother, she is doctor."

He said "is." So his mom is alive. I felt so relieved I took a gulp of water and wolfed down a big forkful of ziti with meat sauce.

"She in Sarajevo," Slobodan said. "She help people hurt in war. In Sarajevo is much fighting, much shooting."

"Will your mom come here?" I asked.

"Yes. When she get visa."

Then Dad had to explain to me that a visa is like a certificate that people from other countries need or America won't let them in.

"When will she get it?"

"One month. Maybe more. Not sure."

Dad said, "You must miss her a lot."

Slobodan looked down at his plate.

I thought, Uh-oh. I was scared he'd start to cry. I sure would, if I had to wait that long. . . .

Slobodan raised his head and said, "You bet!" Then he asked, "Is right? Is how Americans say?"

"You bet! Exactly right!" My father clapped him on the shoulder. "That's just what Americans say."

Then we ate. And when we were done, Slobodan said to my dad, "Now I show you."

He pulled his necktie loose. He opened the top button of his shirt. There was the locket, hanging from a new shoelace. He opened it. "This my mother."

"She's beautiful," said Dad.

"Thank you." Slobodan closed the locket, tucked it back inside his shirt. Then he turned to me. "And thank you also, Shrimp. You know for what."

Dad looked from him to me and asked, "Can I know, too?"

"Was fight today," Slobodan began. "One boy, he try to take locket away. And he make fun about it. But you have brave son, Mr. Pazz—how you say name?"

"Pazzalini," Dad said.

My cheeks started burning. I wanted Dad to find out what I did. But I felt embarrassed just the same.

"Shrimp, he fight with other boy for locket. Then

he give back to me. And he no make fun."

Dad looked me in the eyes. "That was brave, all right." The way he said it made me feel about ten feet tall.

I was also proud of Slobodan for not saying who tried to take the locket away. He's from a whole different part of the world. But one thing is the same—you don't tell on a guy. Even if he's awful and you don't like him.

Speaking of the devil . . . guess who walked in *just* at that moment?

Not the devil, but close—Mike Donnelly, with his whole family.

"Hey, Shrimp!" He waved to me. When he saw who was sitting next to me, his eyes got big and he grinned really wide.

I knew what Mike was thinking as plain as if he said it out loud, Shrimp and Slob-o! Well, isn't that nice.

I could already hear Mike laughing and saying to everyone at school, "Hey guys, guess who Shrimp's new best friend is—Slob-o!" And DeVonn and everybody would be laughing it up.

For about one second I felt like diving under the table. Then I waved back with just as big a grin. "Hey, Mike!" And I moved my chair closer to Slobodan's.

12 DROOG

THAT NIGHT WAS Slobodan's lucky night—and not just because the dinner was so great. When he got home, his mom called. He hadn't heard her voice in four months!

She said she was still waiting for her visa. She still didn't know how long it would take. But the great news was that she was in Zagreb. That's a big city in Croatia, away from the war. No shooting, no bombs. She was safe now. And she could telephone easily from there, so at least they could talk to each other.

Mike was wrong if he told kids that Slob-o and I were best friends. You don't get to be best friends with somebody five inches taller and three years older than you. Especially somebody who speaks a language you don't even know.

But he was speaking English better and better. And I learned a few words in his language, like:

Da. Easy, that means "yes."

Gospodin. "Mister."

Gospoda. "Mrs."

Dobro utro. "Good morning."

He even came over to my house for dinner.

Luckily he didn't have to eat my dad's cooking. My mom was back from Florida! She made chicken and polenta—his favorite dish, Slobodan said. And he ate up a storm.

My mom really took to him.

I made a bet with myself about what she'd say when I told her his name: "How beautiful. It sounds like music."

Ninety-nine percent correct! "How beautiful. It sounds so melodious!" is what she said.

It does sound kind of nice when you say it right. But it *is* long. So I started calling him Dan for short. He liked that okay. And pretty soon other kids called him that, too.

One time when Dan and I were shooting baskets, he asked me, "You not mind kids call you Shrimp?"

Before I knew it, I said, "No." I was kind of surprised. But it was true, I didn't mind it that much anymore. I'm short. So what? One of these days I'll grow. And anyway, I've been feeling taller lately, especially when I hang around with Dan.

Two weeks after we went to Luigi's, Dan got skipped—way up to fifth grade, the highest grade in our school. I was sorry not to have him in our class anymore. But now he could be with kids his own age.

Oh, I almost forgot. I learned another word in his

language, *drug*. Not like headache pills or bad drugs. The way you say it is "droog." It means "friend."

That's what we are, friends. We still hang around with each other after school sometimes. And if kids think we look funny together, him so tall and me so short, who cares? Let 'em laugh!